I0841121

Cut By: _____

His name is Saiku. He is a data analyst and report programmer for a major TV network. He is from a middle class upbringing. His parents died in a car accident when he was very young. He was raised by his uncle. Saiku practices meditation and yoga, and is into Eastern Philosophy. He is fluent in several languages. Saiku wants to better the world through helping others by volunteering for charity causes. He is fairly apolitical but has an uncanny sense for justice. Saiku is a pescatarian.

Her name is Satya. She works at an organic vegan fast food joint part of a worldwide chain. Satya is the daughter of a Telecom tycoon. Her mom, who was a free spirit and who named her, died when she was born. She was raised by her nanny. Satya is fluent in several languages, and accomplished in martial arts. She is a rebel. Left home early in her life to fend for herself as she disagreed with her dad's vision of media control and manipulation. She belongs to a group of activists fighting for social issues and income equality. Satya is vegan.

Both hope that the processed foods complex will cease to exist soon.

They are incredibly sharp individuals but also somewhat absentminded, forgetful and dreamy.

The time is somewhere in the near future. The place, a major metropolis. Even though they do not know each other, their lives follow a sort of parallel track.

It's a Monday morning; they both overslept and are late for work. Getting ready in a rush. They both ride motorcycles.

SPACE CASE
Words/Melody: Rivera & Seda
Music: No Matter What!

I wake up in the morning and I look at myself (yawn)
I don't know what the time is but for sure I am late (oh, oh)
I take a speedy shower and get ready to leave
then suddenly I realize I can't find my keys (Where are my keys?)

I'm looking in the closet, I look under the bed (They're not here)
they're nowhere to be found so I have breakfast instead (chomp, chomp)
I'm opening the freezer, need to get me some ice
and there they are my keys, (My keys!) why is it I'm not surprised?
(Why am I not surprised?)

I'm a Space Case "Space Case" (Oh my god! he's such a Space Case)
I don't know how I got to this place
I'm a Space Case "Space Case" (Such a Space Case!)
but I am not from outer space (Nah-ah, not from outer space)
I'm a Space Case "Space Case"
excuse me I don't remember your face (Who are you anyway?)

I'm a Space Case "Space Case" (brrrip)
my mind is in a permanent daze (wooooshh)

They tell me I have severe ADD (ADD)
It might be time to pop some pills (Yeah! pop some pills)
But I don't like medication
I'd rather do meditation and chill (Chill)

I'm a Space Case "Space Case" (Oh god! he's such a Space Case)
I don't know how I got to this place
I'm a Space Case "Space Case" (Say what?)
but I am not from outer space
(I'm not from outer space!! I'm not from outer space!!!)
I'm a Space Case "Space Case"
excuse me I don't remember your face
I'm a Space Case "Space Case" (Such a Space Case)
my mind is in a permanent daze (Permanent daze)

(Trumpet Solo)

(You're a Space Case man, such a Space Case! Ow, Space Case!
He's such a Space Case. Wait no, that's me: I'm such a Space Case
Man, where are the keys anyway? Can't find them!)

I'm running out the door I'm getting into my car (Vroom, vroom, vroom)
I feel I forgot something but I do not know what
I see my tank is empty I stop for some gasoline
I think it is quite crazy just how cold the ground feels (brrrrrrr)

A man starts talking to me, he seems to know me well (Who is that?)
we chat for a few minutes and he goes on his way (Bye bye)
I wonder who that was I can't remember his face (Oh well!)
why he kept looking at my feet? I don't understand
(Oh, maybe 'cause I'm not wearing shoes?!)

I'm a Space Case "Space Case" (Such a Space Case)
I don't know how I got to this place
I'm a Space Case "Space Case" (You're a Space Case!)
but I am not from outer space
(No I'm not from outer space, I'm from "In Space")
I'm a Space Case "Space Case"
excuse me I don't remember your face (Who are you?)
I'm a Space Case "Space Case" (Say what?)
my mind is in a permanent daze (wooooshh!)

They tell me I have severe ADD (brip, brup)
It might be time to pop some pills (Yeah right!)

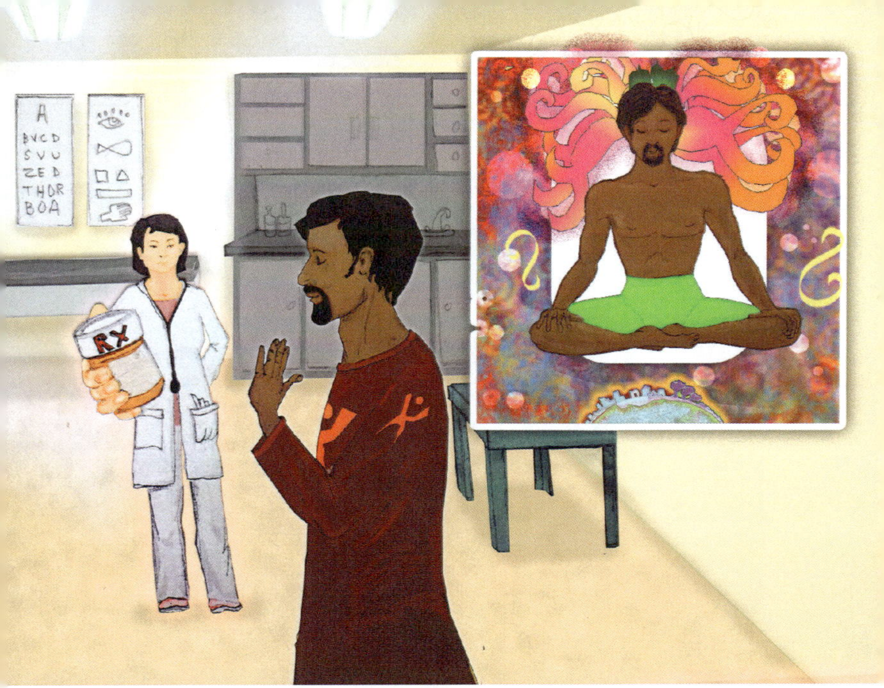
A
BVCD
SVU
ZED
THOR
BOA
RX
??!

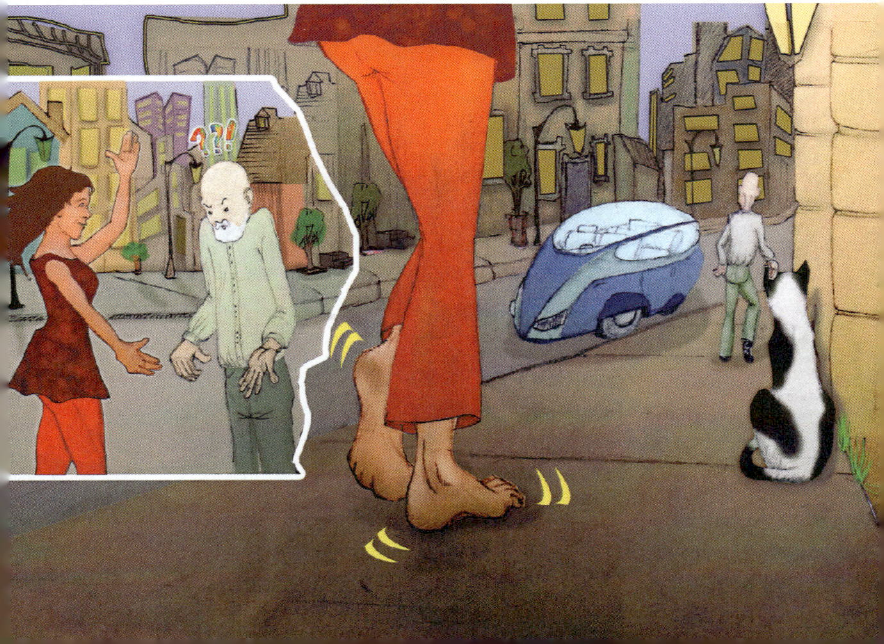

Mc
Vegan
Mc
Vegan
Mc
Vegan

But I don't like medication (Pop some pills)
I'd rather do meditation and chill (OM)

I'm a Space Case "Space Case"
I don't know how I got to this place (Yeah! whatever)
I'm a Space Case "Space Case"
but I am not from outer space (Outer space?)
I'm a Space Case "Space Case" (Such a... Space Case)
excuse me I don't remember your face
(Space Case, Space Case, Space Case)
I'm a Space Case "Space Case"
my mind is in a permanent daze (blip, blup, brup, brip)

What is it that I was supposed to be doing here?
Space Case
I think I came here for some milk
Space Case
Oh No! (Not again!)
Space Case
I took the wrong freeway again!
Space Case, "Space Case"

Saiku learns through his gay co-worker best friend: Huiliang, that he is being considered for a promotion. Saiku is called into the boss's office and is offered a huge salary increase and more responsibility. He does not understand how the network can afford this when they're operating in the red. He is told that there will be massive layoffs and his first task is to do the firings. Saiku is also told that the employees with the higher seniority and benefits will all be axed. Huiliang's name is on the list! Saiku presents a savings plan that will bring numbers back to black through salary reduction of high management positions and energy efficiency; and without layoffs! He is told his plan won't work and to do as told or leave the company. He feels nauseated and quits!

Satya finds out that the supposed organic vegan fast food chain she works for actually produces some of their dishes using a banned animal fat. She is outraged and confronts the manager about it. Satya explains that there are viable real vegan alternatives that are even less expensive. She is told the chain has billion dollar contracts with the manufacturers of those deceiving products. He tells her to keep it low or he'll fire her. She tells him to fuck off and she quits!!

DON'T TAKE IT NO MORE
Words/Melody: Rivera & Seda
Music: No Matter What!

The economy is in crisis, the company downsizes
and loyalty means nothing when it's time to save a buck

The new CEO yelling, says we're a bunch of idiots
the ones that don't get fired, get their salary cut

We're told there's a line of people waiting to take our positions
we must be more productive with less pay, there's no excuse
And here we are complaining about our situation
we fool ourselves by thinking there is nothing to do

The voice in my head is growing stronger
it's telling me it's time to rise and be gone
I must put an end to injustice
get up and leave this hellhole once and for all

Don't take it no more... don't take it no more... don't take it no more!!

(Trumpet Solo)

We have become complacent, our dignity has faded
Our benefits are taken, they keep milking our fear
A voice inside is shouting in deep rage and frustration
it is begging me to wake up and set myself free

So screw the corporation, greedy-ass board of directors
whose only concern is profit and the new toys they can buy
Why wait 'til I am older, to wish I'd done it sooner
Must take a leap of faith and live a dream that is mine

The voice in my head is growing stronger
it's telling me it's time to rise and be gone
I must put an end to injustice
get up and leave this hellhole once and for all

Don't take it no more... don't take it no more... don't take it no more!!

The voice in our heads is growing stronger
it's telling us it's time to rise and be gone
We must put an end to injustice
get up and leave this hellhole once and for all

Don't take it no more... don't take it no more... don't take it no more!!

Satya and Saiku feel uncertain without a job. Huiliang invites Saiku to a demonstration at the public square. A peaceful gathering pro-minorities' and undocumented immigrants' causes. Huiliang, besides being gay, is also undocumented as he was brought to the country by his parents when he was a baby.

As fate would have it, Satya attends the demonstration as well with her best friend: Tacari. He is a black gay young man who is very lighthearted; he jokes around all the time and is immediately loved by all who meet him. Tacari is also fiery and feisty.

WWWEEEOOO

A brawl ensues between a so-called "white" nationalist and Tacari. Even though he does not know Tacari, Huiliang jumps into the fight and they are both being beat up pretty badly.

Satya notices what is going on and jumps into the fight as well. She is a top-notch martial artist and takes over the situation starting to subdue the so-called Nationalist and his friends. Saiku is coming back from getting snacks and jumps into the fight as well, but his intention is to stop it. In the process he puts himself in harm's way to protect Satya from a rubber bullet, which knocks him out. Police arrive and the fight breaks off.

Saiku recovers consciousness inside the police van. Satya, Tacari, Huiliang and him, are being taken to the police station with the nationalist.

Huiliang is tending to Tacari's wounds. Satya thanks Saiku for taking the rubber bullet for her. He thanks her for defending their friends. Electric sparks fill the air.

Saiku talks to the so-called white nationalist. His name is Aitan. Saiku asks him if he is OK while examining his wounds. He explains the inability of minorities in most cases to have a say in their situation. Aitan is going through a horrible time. He was laid off and lost his house and family to the recent economic depression. Even though he is fully aware of the faults of government and tyranny of corporate rule, Aitan has been convinced through propaganda (and truly believes) that the minorities and undocumented immigrants are at fault.

Saiku explains that it's in fact the corporate ruling elite, playing the "divide and conquer" card super effectively, who is at fault and that all go through the same plight regardless of race or origin. They seem to reach an understanding. The other three are dumbfounded at how easy it had been to communicate. They all agree to stay in touch.

IN TOLERANCE
Words/Melody: Rivera & Seda
Music: No Matter What!

Are we in tolerance, or are we intolerant?

Wars are waged because intolerance rules our heads
Fear born from ignorance so quick turns into hate
Are we misguided by the dogma shoved down our throats?
What does it take to learn that tolerance equals love?

When we take some time to know those we think we loathe
we will discover that they're more like us than we thought
Religion, sexual orientation, gender, color of skin
or nationality, not valid to provoke hate within

If we're gay: "promiscuous!" No!!
If we're dark: "we're thugs!" No!!
If we're white: "we're racist!" No!!
If we're Muslim: "terrorist!" No!!
If pro-choice, "we're killers!" No!!
If pro-life, "fanatics!" No!!
If we're rich, "we're greedy!" No!!
If we're poor, "we're lazy!" No!!
If immigrant, "illegal!" No!!
If tattooed, "a gangster!" No!!

Is it really crazy to keep wishing for…
Peaceful coexistence without the hatred,
without the judgment, without the fear?

Are we in tolerance, or are we intolerant?

Tolerance, intolerance which do we choose?
Make a conscious effort or else we lose

(Guitar Solo)

Judging and demonizing those who judge and condemn
perpetuates the very cycle we wish to break
But tolerance requires inconceivable strength
self-control is so much harder than turning violent

If we're gay: "promiscuous!" No!!
If we're dark: "we're thugs!" No!!
If we're white: "we're racist!" No!!
If we're Muslim: "terrorist!" No!!
If pro-choice, "we're killers!" No!!
If pro-life, "fanatics!" No!!
If immigrant, "illegal!" No!!
If tattooed, "a gangster!"

Can't we wish for peaceful coexistence
without the fear?

Are we in tolerance, or are we intolerant?

It is not a question of who's right or wrong
That's not the point at all

Tolerance, intolerance which do we choose?
Make a conscious effort or else we lose

Are we in tolerance, or are we intolerant?
What the fuck do we choose? Keep your cool

Saiku is thinking a lot about Satya. She thinks a lot about him as well. Tacari and Huiliang think about each other too. Saiku has so many plans and so does Satya. Both have had their share of heartbreak in their lives, and are incredibly hesitant to get involved in a new relationship. Yet, both feel incredibly energized by their recent encounter and with a new zest for life.

Saiku talks it over with his uncle who raised him and taught him meditation. He hopes his uncle will clearly tell him which way to go, but he is told to listen to his intuition and follow his heart.

Satya consults with her nanny who raised her. She also hopes to get clear direction from her, but the latter says that while it seems as though Saiku has a gentle soul, she should follow her heart and not force anything.

While both are doubtful, something inside tells them to forget the past and jump again into the unknown and unpredictable ways of love.

GO FOR IT

Words/Melody: Rivera & Seda
Music: No Matter What!

I realize I'm running like a chicken
with its head cut-off
I never stop, I'm getting lost
in trivial, unimportant small stuff

I feel that my life slips away
like sand between my fingers
and the feeling lingers
while I see that none of my dreams
have become true

I've been searching too long for an answer
and there's not much left to think anymore
Now is the time to forget limitations
demolish the fears 'cuz I am in control
No time to waste dreaming of possibilities
life doesn't stop! when I'm asleep

The call's for action without distraction
Be mindful, be focused and go for it
Don't wait 'til it's too late, no!!

I feel this energy running through my spine
it fills me up and makes me feel alive
Procrastination gone and forgotten
belongs in the past, I'm not looking back

The air I'm breathing, the ground under my feet,
this moment I'm living is what's all about

The call's for action without distraction
Be mindful, be focused and go for it
The time to act is right now!!

(Trumpet Interlude)

Excuse after excuse I try to justify
why I cannot get off my ass
The reasons why keep piling up
behind my own eyes

It's like I'm sabotaging all my dreams
Why can't I see it starts with me?
There's no one else, nor circumstances
to be blamed at all

I've been searching too long for an answer
and there's not much left to think anymore
Now is the time to forget limitations
demolish the fears 'cuz I am in control
No time to waste dreaming of possibilities
life doesn't stop! when I'm asleep

The call's for action without distraction
Be mindful, be focused and go for it
Don't wait 'til it's too late, no!!

I feel this energy running through my spine
it fills me up and makes me feel alive
Procrastination gone and forgotten
belongs in the past, I'm not looking back
The air I'm breathing, the ground under my feet,
this moment I'm living is what's all about

The call's for action without distraction
Be mindful, be focused and go for it
The time to act is right now!!

(Trumpet Solo)

Go For It! Don't wait 'til it's too late, no!!

I feel this energy running through my spine
it fills me up and makes me feel alive
Procrastination gone and forgotten
belongs in the past, I'm not looking back
The air I'm breathing, the ground under my feet,

FAST TRANSIT
STRESS
100P

this moment I'm living is what's all about
The call's for action without distraction
Be mindful, be focused and Go For It!

Both Satya and Saiku receive a mysterious text message invitation to a gathering about anti-war/pro-peace causes and activism. It turns out that the invite came from Aitan! They expect to find a pretty homogenous group of white people at the event but to their surprise, the gathering is incredibly diverse with people from all walks of life. Tacari and Huiliang also attend the meeting.

Even though the various groups in attendance fight for different and seemingly opposing causes, they all agree that the waste and abuse by the military industrial complex in the name of democracy and freedom has drained the country of resources and affects them all equally while benefiting only a few. There is an "Elders Council" whose members are the leaders of the various individual groups.

A group of ex-soldiers expounds the atrocities committed abroad by their country's military against otherwise peaceful peoples.

IN THE NAME OF PEACE
Words/Melody: Rivera & Seda
Music: No Matter What!

Our taxes sponsoring destruction
across the globe they're spreading death & fear
While we don't take care of our needy
They're lonely, getting raped on city streets

Evil men hide in the dark
Their war machine victims
are children who die

The Media is complicit in their plan
While they live lavish wasted lives
Our young are sent yet one more time to fight
A crisis of "humanitarian" lies
There's blood in their lies

When the wars are fought
In the name of peace
The one and only goal
Is feeding empires of greed
In the name of peace

(Trumpet & Guitar Soli)

Evil men hide in the dark
Their war machine victims
are children who die

Geopolitics and full control
of others' natural resources
They also want to control human lives
Red stain on a spotless bed of their lies
There's blood in their lies

When the wars are fought
In the name of peace
The one and only goal
Is feeding empires of...

When the wars are fought
In the name of peace
The one and only goal
Is feeding empires of greed
In the name of peace

When the wars are fought...

In the name of peace!

They all leave the meeting with a newfound sense of fraternity and connected-
ness. Even the most extreme nationalists understand that the economic struggle
the immigrants face is the same as theirs. The minorities also understand that the
source of the nationalists' hatred towards them is the economic struggle they all
face equally. They seem to have found common ground in the anti-war sentiment.

After the meeting, Satya and Saiku find themselves alone on a rooftop. Words
are few and looks are deep. A soul connection, something neither experienced
before, takes place. Magic fills the air. They kiss and the world with its myriad of
problems is forgotten for a moment that seems to last forever, yet too short.

A similar situation happens between Tacari and Huiliang in a different setting.

BOSSAMBALA

Music: No Matter What!

Six months later, Satya is with Tacari at a vegan cafe. They're talking about their
new relationships and how happy they are. Tacari tells Satya that it would be good if
she could devote more time to the local minority oppression issues which are more
<<real>> to them, and stop spending so much time on foreign wars issues which
are rather removed from their everyday lives. She disagrees explaining to him that
both issues are deeply interconnected as these foreign wars are usually waged in
places where the affected populations are minorities. Also, the cost of war affects

HOLLYWOOD
MORE MORE MORE

NOOO

minorities and lower classes in general as it results in lack of resources for local programs of social uplift.

All of a sudden, a group of homophobic bigots comes into the Café and starts disrupting the peace by harassing an inter-racial couple of lesbian women. Tacari cannot contain himself anymore and faces the hoodlums, telling them to go fuck themselves!

FIGHT & DON'T BACK DOWN
Words/Melody: Rivera & Seda
Music: No Matter What!

[This is the tale of Naila]
This is the tale of a girl
A girl whose name is Naila, and when she…
When she was eight *[She was bullied when she was eight]*
she was bullied
By two shy twisted sisters who were twins *[Twisted indeed]*

They sat her down, on the green grass
In front of her a smelly cow-dung pile *[Guacala!]*
They were so mean, they told her "eat it" *[Blargh!]*
Naila wouldn't despite fearing consequence

There was no way on Earth she'd eat that shite
She held her head always high
from that day on she would never bow down
to tyranny again

Now Naila is with The People *[She's with The People]* "With The People!"
And the bully is much bigger and stronger
A conglomerate of nefarious powers at work

Naila Fight & Don't Back Down
Fight, don't back down! Fight!

Tacari is confident that Satya will have his back, knowing she is a master of Capoeira but to his surprise she advises to keep calm and call the police. Satya is trying to avert the fight by telling Tacari that she is not his savior, that she cannot fight his fights and that peace through dialog should prevail. Tacari is furious and tells Satya that she has been influenced too much by Saiku and that she has lost perspective. Tacari attacks the group of bigots and a fight ensues. Unexpectedly, Tacari is clobbered on the head and he ends up in an indefinite coma at the Hospital.

Tacari's dad, a fundamentalist minister who despises the LGBT community, just learned about his son's sexual orientation. He blames Satya and forbids her from visiting him. Satya is devastated and decides to forget about the anti-war cause and refocus on local issues as Tacari wanted. Saiku wholeheartedly disagrees and they get into a HUGE argument.

THE SONG OF WRONG
Words/Melody: Rivera & Seda
Music: No Matter What!

I'm always right / You're never right
You're always wrong / I'm never wrong
You're never right / I'm always right
I'm never wrong / You're always wrong

You say I sound so righteous
and when you say so you sound righteous to me
I think I'm going crazy
well, crazy is the only way I can be

I'm always wrong / You're never wrong
You're always right / I'm never right
You're never wrong / I'm always wrong
I'm never right / You're always right

I say you sound so righteous
and when I say so I sound righteous to you
You think you're going crazy
well, crazy is the only way to get through

We're always right (Damn right!)
They're always wrong
They're never right, (No, No!)
We're never wrong, wrong, wrong, wrong, wrong,
    wrong, wrong, wrong, wrong
That's right! (One more time)

(Trumpet & Guitar soli)

Oh what the fuck is going on?
Can you not see that you're so wrong?
Have you gone mad are you insane?
Why do you keep pulling my chain?

You say I sound so righteous
and when you say so you sound righteous to me
I think I'm going crazy
well, crazy is the only way I can be

Oh yes you're right / You are insane
I am the one / That pulls my chain

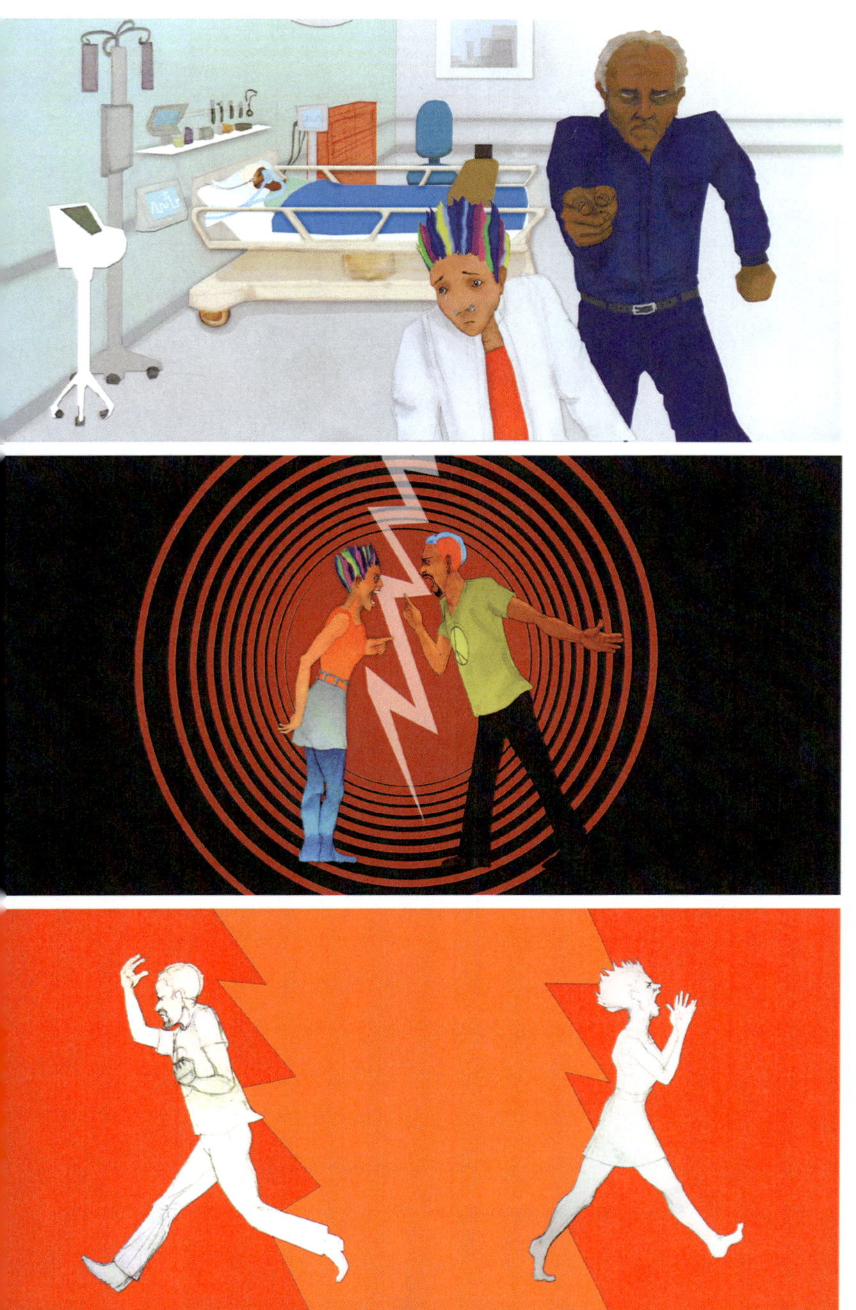

SATYA
Truth & Integrity
in Sanskrit

SAIKU
Prudent & Wise
in Egyptian Hieroglyphics

SELAM
Peace
in Amharic

AITAN
Strong
in Hebrew

ITZEL
Rainbow
Goddess
in Mayan

HUILIANG
Kind & Good
in Chinese

TACARI
Warrior
in African Dialect

So wrong I am / There is no hope
I'm such a fool / Oh what a dope!

I say you sound so righteous
and when I say so I sound righteous to you
You think you're going crazy
well, crazy is the only way to get through

We're always right (Damn right!)
They're always wrong
They're never right, (No, no!)
We're never wrong, wrong, wrong, wrong, wrong, wrong, wrong, wrong

That's just wrong… Seriously though

Satya and Saiku break up and emotional misery befalls both of them. They wander alone, sad and lost, taking refuge in the activist groups they belong to. They also blame each other for their intransigence and inability to reach a compromise.

PEOPLE FUCK UP!
Words/Melody: Rivera & Seda
Music: No Matter What!

People fuck up, friends let you down
You never know, who'll come around

Sometimes we think we know someone
we set our expectations high
Look out! It may all be in our minds
they might not know what we really want

We set ourselves up again *[We set ourselves up again]*
for disappointment and pain
It sure seems we haven't learned *[for disappointment and pain]*
about the rules of this game

Desires and fear must end *[When are we gonna understand]*
before we can be content
When are we gonna understand *[that it's on us not on them]*
that it's on us and not on them? (when)...

People fuck up, friends let you down
You never know, who'll come around

We think our friends and family'll come through
as we face life's most challenging truths
Sometimes we may be surprised
to find a stranger's helping hand

A stranger becomes a friend *[A stranger becomes a friend]*
suddenly life's good again
Anxiety didn't pay *[Suddenly life's good again]*
it was such a big fucking waste
The voices in our heads screamed *[It's not always what it seems]*
but it was all just a dream
It's not always what it seems *[There's no black or white extremes]*
there's no black or white extremes (when)…

People fuck up, friends let you down
You never know, who'll come around

People fuck up, friends let you down
You never know, who will come around
People fuck up, you never know

You never know, you never know who'll come around

A few months later Satya and Saiku continue to be fully focused on their separate (while intrinsically related) causes. Each still blaming the other for their emotional sorrow.

By chance Satya meets a very young woman online. The girl's name is Selam and she has managed to break through an Internet ban in her far away country. She is reaching out for help. It turns out she lives in one of those countries plagued by wars for natural resources since the time before she was born. Selam's only hope is for peace and finding a better life. Despite her plight she is aware that the people in the country whose military has invaded hers are not at fault, at least not in a conscious way. Selam shares a gruesome video and stories that make Satya incredibly sorrowful and which renew in her the conviction that wars of aggression committed by her country in the name of supposed peace and freedom go against any social equality she is fighting for locally.

YEARNING FOR PEACE (WAR CHILD)
Words/Melody: Rivera & Seda ~ Final quote: Amy Goodman
Music: No Matter What!

I find myself playing in the backyard with my dolls. I'm in the tree house my daddy built for me; the sun peeks through the window

I take a deep breath and enjoy the sound of the singing birds. I climb down the tree and play with my baby cat; I hug him close to my heart

Out of nowhere, a thundering explosion wakes me up and throws me back into reality

My name means peace, but I don't know what that is…

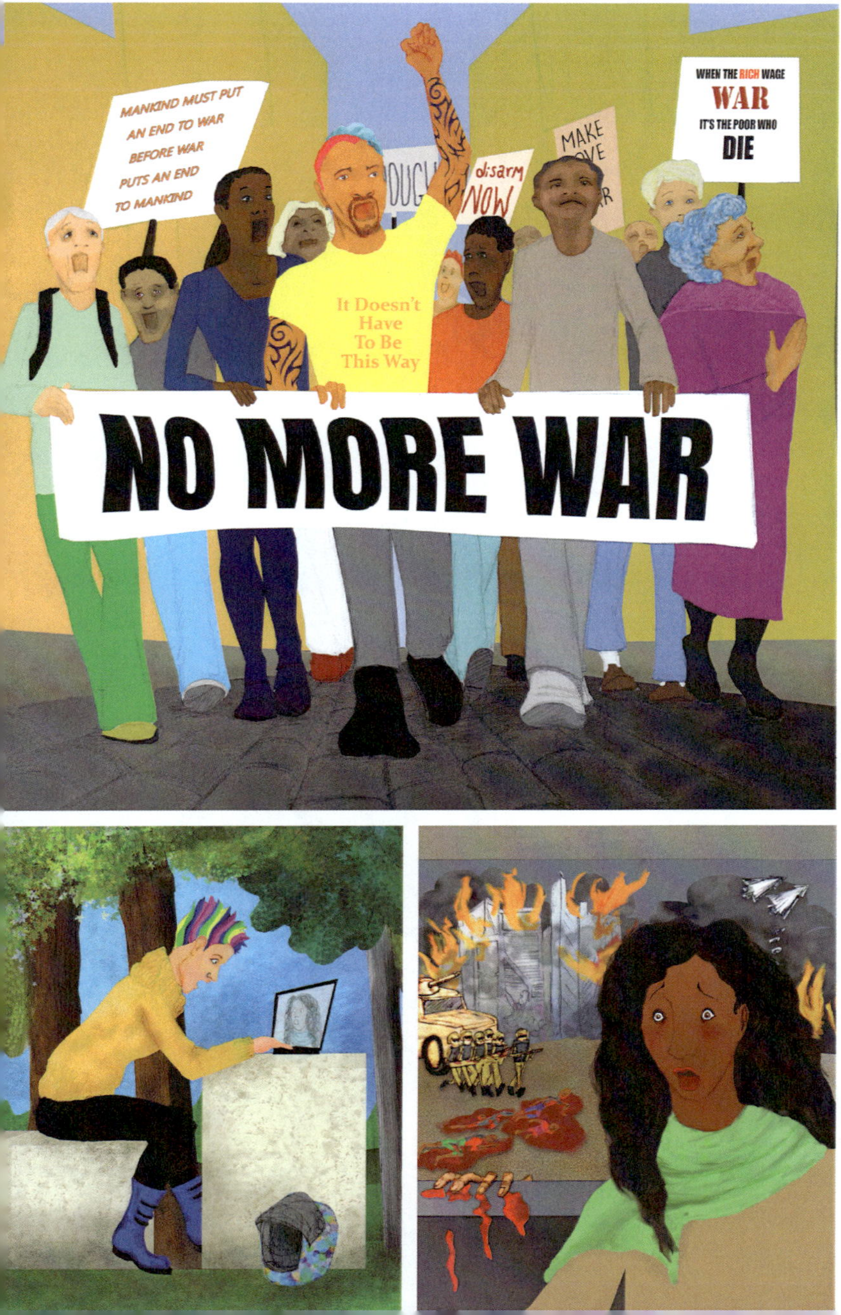

Yearning for the peace I've never known (yearning for peace)
Yearning for the peace I've never known (yearning for peace)
Yearning for the peace I've never known (yearning for peace)
Yearning for Peace!

War Child: This is the life that I know
I'm a War Child. War! The only world that I know

Living in this country by war torn
from before the time when I was born
Saw so much war before I turned four
inside I feel so numb I can't cry no more

I wish the world could see
what a shameful disgrace
human rights abuses
here are commonplace

I saw them shoot my dad and rape my mom
Where are my brothers now? Forever gone!
Seen so many children in terror scream
running for their lives with a shattered dream
Bullets in return for throwing rocks
Violence, more violence. Will it ever stop?

You can get a child out of the war but never get the war out of a child.
An eye for an eye and soon the whole world will be blind;
but I want to see and be free of…

War Child. War! This is the life that I know
I'm a War Child. War! The only world that I know

(Trumpet & Guitar Soli)

Yearning for the peace I've never known (yearning for peace)
Yearning for the peace I've never known (yearning for peace)
Yearning for the peace I've never known (yearning for peace)
Yearning for Peace!

War Child: This is the life that I know
I'm a War Child. War! The only world that I know

Building up inside me all this hate
Tell me how I can make it dissipate?
We fight for our land, not follow commands
defend our family, peace buried in sand
How can we be healed from all this grief?
Release us from this ever-growing pattern of disease

Is it even possible to coexist?
What has to be changed to cease and desist?
If the world could see, compassion would increase
Is it really feasible to live in peace?
Who will take the first step towards non-violence?
Civil disobedience, does it make any sense?

Maybe once we realize we're all human,
we can start living together instead of killing each other

"Could you imagine if, for just one week, we saw the images of war
every day: a photograph and story about a soldier dead and dying; a
baby dead on the ground; or a family maybe killed by a drone attack;
or a woman with her legs blown off by cluster bombs? Americans are
a compassionate people, they would say: No! War is not the answer to
conflict in the 21st century"

Satya reaches out to Saiku to share Selam's stories and video, since he is still
actively part of the anti-war / pro-peace movement. They have a long conversation
about their involvement in their separate causes. He asks her how Tacari is doing.
She says he is still in a coma and his dad is still forbidding her to visit him.

While electricity and emotional tension fill the air, both are too proud to admit
they miss each other. Finally, Saiku brings up the issue and asks how she is doing
otherwise. He opens up and tells her that he is deeply sorry they broke up. He is
surprised to learn that she feels the same way and asks her if she thinks it would
be worthwhile to try to mend their relationship and give it another go. They have a
long talk about how things evolved, recognize each other's past inability to listen
and decide to try again.

BEFORE THE LOVE HAS GONE
Words/Melody: Rivera & Seda
Music: No Matter What!

It seems like yesterday
when we first met each other
We quickly became friends
before we knew it we were lovers

It was a permanent high
We couldn't get enough of one another
We never took time apart
spent every single minute together
Moved in together so quickly
just after a few moons

ELEC
30%

Guess we got closer too fast
maybe too close too soon

Things became intense
Tension built up like boiling water
Got on each other's nerves
and yelling replaced the laughter

So where do we go from here?

Before the love has gone away
so much left to create, please stay
How can we work it out and save
the love that we still have today

(Flügel Horn Solo)

Let's remind each other
that what we have is precious
that we can ask for help
when the times are stressful

And stop the crazy arguments
over meaningless things
No more calling names
no more rage and no more hate
Even though it might take some time
it is not yet too late
You are the love of my life
I keep reminding myself

You're my friend not my enemy
so let us not lose the hope we've got
And let's keep close every day and night
let us stop all the senseless fights

Can we try and see the light?

Before the love has gone away
so much left to create, please stay
How can we work it out and save
the love that we still have today?
Before the love has gone away
True love never goes away. Relationships transform. Yeah! They change

After Satya and Saiku watch Selam's video footage, they clearly understand the underlying unity of peoples across the globe and the world-wide repercussions of their country's military actions at the command of a savage ruling elite who owns the corrupt government. A war machine funded by a vast portion of the taxes that

Satya, Saiku and their fellow compatriots pay, while scant resources are allocated to programs for the common benefit.

In addition, Satya has just come across a confidential video in which a group of influential and well-known politicians as well as members of the ruling class are planning the next wars of aggression for control of natural resources. Some of these individuals are famous people from the entertainment and news media industries who are beloved by the majority of the common folk. It's clear that this group despises the lower classes regardless of origin, race, religion, sexual orientation etc., and that their only preoccupation is with having more power and more money to live empty, lavish, wasteful lives.

Satya and Saiku decide to share Selam's story and both videos with the anti-war/pro-peace underground group at their next secret meeting.

At the meeting, one of the council elders, a kind woman named Itzel informs all that a hacker from her group has been developing a worldwide reaching program that has the ability to overtake all networks and means of communication for a short period. She suggests sharing the info presented by Satya using this tool so peoples around the world are made aware and, who knows, maybe a worldwide peaceful uprising could take place.

The other elder council members are fearful that exposing their network may end up damaging the ground they've gained so far. The council advises against sharing Selam's story and video footage, as well as the other video.

Both Satya and Saiku are perplexed and do not understand how such a golden opportunity can be wasted. They appeal one more time to the council.

WALK LIKE WE TALK
Words/Melody: Rivera & Seda
Music: No Matter What!

To walk like we talk we must have the guts
To do what it takes need not be afraid

We say that we found our calling
at last the dream we'd been searching
Tired of the same old story
now we're ready to go for it
Willing to do what it takes

No matter what's in the way
No matter what's in the way

But our words are sounding empty
the drive is lacking in our actions

N
NO
NO

wait no wait no
wait no wa
wait no wa
wait no
wa
no
wait no
wait no
wa
wait
no
it no
it no
no

Talk with no work the world has plenty
we just don't seem to have the passion

It seemed we had a common dream
something so rare to find in life
But I guess that we were blinded
blinded by our own excitement

Should have seen the signs much earlier
have we been wasting all this time?
Spinning our wheels in the same place
getting nowhere really fast

To walk like we talk we must have the guts
To do what it takes need not be afraid
To walk like we talk we need intense drive
A burning desire to give it a try

(Bass interlude)

We say that we found our calling
at last the dream we'd been searching
Tired of the same old story
now we're ready to go for it
Willing to do what it takes

No matter what's in the way
No matter what's in the way

But our words are sounding empty
the drive is lacking in our actions
Talk with no work the world has plenty
we just don't seem to have the passion

To walk like we talk we must have the guts
To do what it takes need not be afraid
To walk like we talk we need intense drive
A burning desire to give it a try

To walk like we talk (we must have the guts)
To walk like we talk (to do what it takes)
To walk like we talk (need not be afraid)
To walk like we talk... Oooooo...
we must have the guts!

    Some time goes by and out of nowhere Satya and Saiku are contacted by Itzel. She says that after a long struggle she managed to convince the other council members to concoct a plan for sharing the info with the world. Some people in the group have high technical skills and they have found a way to flood all media outlets including conventional and online means, social media, as well as underground networks with the information, while simultaneously translating it!

They decide to move forward and on a fateful morning the info is presented to the masses around the world. It immediately goes viral and the outrage by the good peoples of all walks of life around the planet is enough to cause a reaction that results in a peaceful uprising against the ruling elites of the world. A peaceful revolution of sorts, conducted both online and on the physical plane, is now underway.

PEOPLE POWER

Words: Rivera, Seda & Carfi
Melody: Rivera & Seda
Music: No Matter What!

People Power
Take a stand and fight the power

In the numbers lies our strength
if we can only do away with self-segregation
Our common goal is clear:
a better life for ourselves in every nation

When you empower yourself you inspire someone else
A chain reaction (takes place)
and people of the world realize that we are all
in this together

Separation is artificial, leads to frustration and isolation

Gimme your cold hand to warm with my hand
you are not a stranger to me: no one is an island
Grassroots is the key, you are here with me
Anything is possible if only we get it, stand here together
against oppressing minds

People Power
Take a stand and fight the power
that constrains your throat
and breathes fear in your ear
Let the fire inspire, take us higher, ignite the desire
of being one people, one race: the human race

People Power
Take a stand and fight the power
People Power

If somebody comes to tell you that the battle can't be won
or that something can't be done, that you believe in

BREAKING NEWS

NO MORE WARS
END ALL WARS
VOS G
NO
MULTILATERAL DECLARATION OF WORLD PEACE
SPECIAL REPORT
THE WARS ARE OVER

Don't be receivin' the lies they be sayin', the truth you be displayin'
like trees swaying in the breeze, bringing them to their knees

We makin' history, and life is just a mystery
and it doesn't have to be so complicated
when the simple truth is navigated with integrity

You see? You and me, we were born free
free as the wind blows and the grass grows
and the people know exactly what they're doing when united

Let the fire of your freedom be ignited, like a flower
Yes! It's time to feel the People Power

(Saz Solo)

Martin Luther King and Gandhi showed
non-violence is the road
that leads to freedom
So let's forget the need
for individual gain and greed
Unite our efforts

Separation is artificial, leads to frustration and isolation

Gimme your cold hand to warm with my hand
you are not a stranger to me: no one is an island
Grassroots is the key, you are here with me
Anything is possible if only we get it, stand here together
against oppressing minds

People Power
Take a stand and fight the power
that constrains your throat
breathes fear in your ear
Let the fire inspire, take us higher, ignite the desire
of being one people, one race: the human race

People Power
Take a stand and fight the power
People Power, People Power, People Power, People Power!

After months of struggle, victory is attained and a period of peace and prosperity for all follows suit. Perpetrators are brought to justice, but no hate is bestowed upon them. The absence of wars results in a better economy now focused on renewable energy, sustainability and the common good. The better economic circumstances make people more peaceful and accepting of others.

Satya manages to sneak Huiliang into the hospital room where Tacari has been laying in a coma for many months now. Saiku is also there for support.

Tacari's dad, who suddenly shows up, is outraged and threatens to call the police to have them all thrown out of the hospital. He is yelling at the top of his voice, blaming them over and over for his son's condition.

Both Satya and Saiku manage to contain the dad while Huiliang talks to Tacari. He is holding his hand; he kisses him gently on the forehead and asks him to please come back. The world is now a better place for them, and he misses him so much!

All of a sudden, through the power of love, Huiliang manages to reach Tacari's subconscious. Tacari opens his eyes! He is extremely weak but fully conscious.

Tacari's dad is so grateful to have his son back that he does not only forgive Satya and her friends, but he also fully understands what just happened and accepts his son's sexual orientation and his relationship with Huiliang.

Tacari, who had always been beloved by all thanks to his kind nature, contagious enthusiasm and sense of humor, asks why everyone looks so happy and if he has missed anything. They all laugh and the room is filled with love, hugs and kisses.

A few hours later, Saiku and Satya are outside of the hospital, which is in the middle of the city. They are standing next to their motorcycles. The clear Sky is a radiant blue and the air feels cleaner for some reason. They look at each other in silence for a long moment, an incredibly big smile on both of their faces. They nod to each other, put their helmets on, jump on their bikes, and ride out of the city and through winding canyon roads as the sun sets on the horizon.

ADRENALIZED FREEDOM
Words: Rivera & Seda
Music: No Matter What!

¡¡Adrenalized Freedom!!

The End

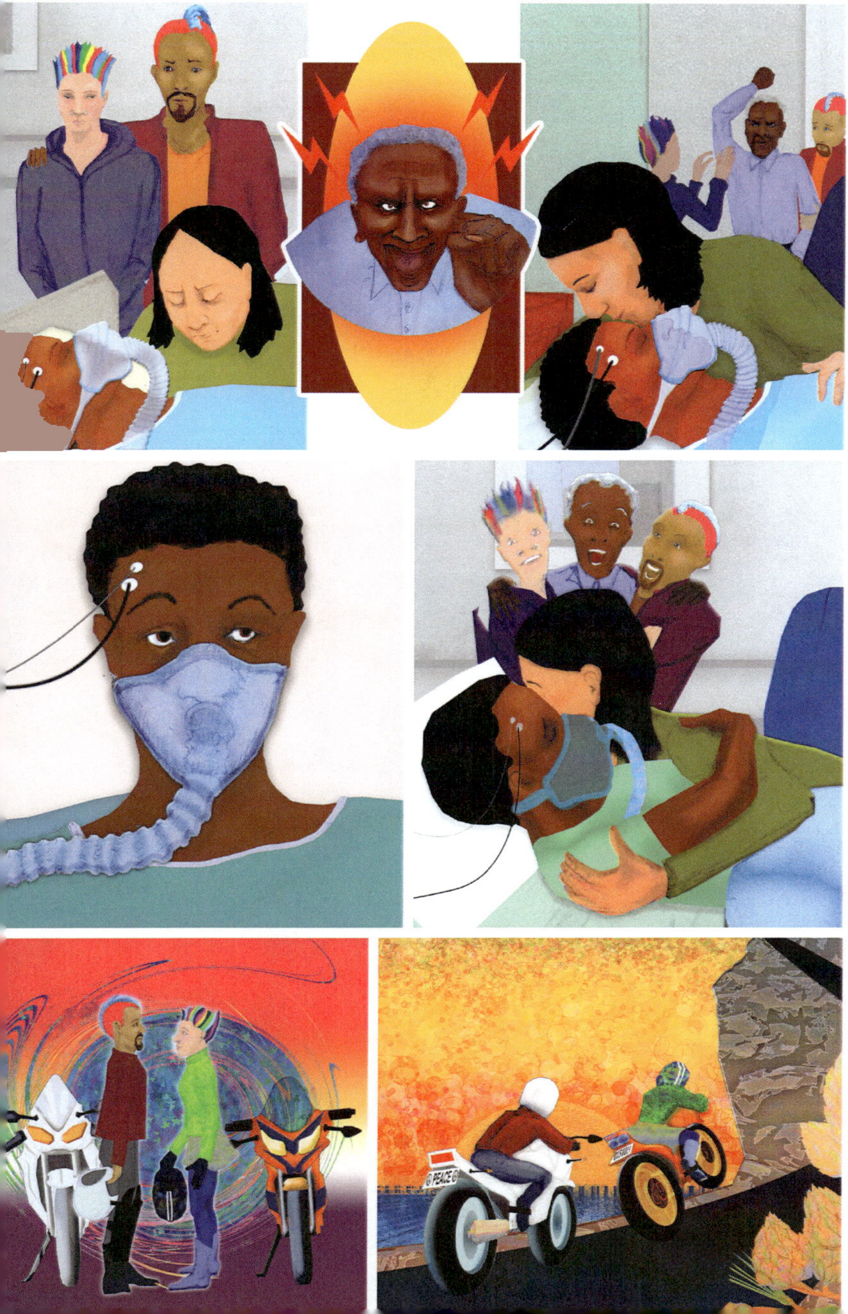

RECORDING CREDITS

All tracks recorded/engineered by Hector Rivera at Riverananda Studios in Los Angeles, California except where otherwise noted.

Story Narration recorded by Carlos Rivera in Puerto Vallarta, Mexico. Edited by Hector Rivera. Mixed by Shawn Lyon.

All tracks produced by Hector Rivera & Mona Seda.

All tracks mixed by Shawn Lyon at his Studios in Los Angeles, California except where otherwise noted.

All tracks mastered by Shawn Lyon at his Studios in Los Angeles, California

SPACE CASE
Mona Seda – Vocals & Trumpet
Hector Rivera – Vocals, Guitar & Drums
Daniele De Cario – Bass

Hector's Guitar recorded/engineered by Jean Luis Contreras at Gracon Studios in Los Angeles, California

DON'T TAKE IT NO MORE
Mona Seda – Vocals & Trumpet
Hector Rivera – Vocals, Guitar, Drums & Bongos
John Carfi – Bass

Drums & Bass recorded/engineered by Dave Beyer at his Studios in Glendale, California

Guitar re-amped by Shawn Lyon at his Studios in Los Angeles, California

IN TOLERANCE
Mona Seda – Vocals & Trumpet
Hector Rivera – Vocals, Guitar & Drums
Daniele De Cario – Bass
Jean Luis Contreras – Guitar

Jean Luis's Guitar recorded/engineered by Jean Luis Contreras at Gracon Studios in Los Angeles, California

GO FOR IT
Mona Seda – Vocals & Trumpet
Hector Rivera – Vocals, Guitar & Drums
Daniele De Cario – Bass

IN THE NAME OF PEACE
Mona Seda – Vocals & Trumpet
Hector Rivera – Vocals & Guitar
Daniele De Cario – Bass
Forrest Robinson – Drums
Mike Basica – Guitar

BOSSAMBALA
Mona Seda – Flügel Horn
Hector Rivera – Guitar & additional Percussion
Daniele De Cario – Bass
Victor Salas – Percussion

Mixed by Hector Rivera at Riverananda Studios in Los Angeles, California

FIGHT & DON'T BACK DOWN
Mona Seda – Vocals & Trumpet
Hector Rivera – Vocals & Guitar
Daniele De Cario – Bass
Forrest Robinson – Drums
Mike Basica – Guitar

THE SONG OF WRONG
Mona Seda – Vocals & Trumpet
Hector Rivera – Vocals & Guitar
Daniele De Cario – Bass
Forrest Robinson – Drums
Mike Basica – Guitar

PEOPLE FUCK UP
Mona Seda – Vocals
Hector Rivera – Vocals, Guitar & Drums
Daniele De Cario – Bass

YEARNING FOR PEACE (WAR CHILD)
Mona Seda – Vocals & Trumpet
Hector Rivera – Vocals & Guitar
Daniele De Cario – Bass
Forrest Robinson – Drums
Mike Basica – Guitar
Samantha Rojas – Intro Voice
Amy Goodman – Final Quote

BEFORE THE LOVE HAS GONE
Mona Seda – Vocals & Flügel Horn
Hector Rivera – Vocals, Guitar & additional Drums
Daniele De Cario – Bass
Kim Diaz – Drums
Mike Basica – Guitar

WALK LIKE WE TALK
Mona Seda – Vocals & Trumpet
Hector Rivera – Vocals & Guitar
Daniele De Cario – Bass
Kim Diaz – Drums
Mike Basica – Guitar

PEOPLE POWER
Mona Seda – Vocals & Trumpet
Hector Rivera – Vocals, Guitar & Drums
John Carfi – Rap Vocals
Daniele De Cario – Bass
Forrest Robinson – Dumbek
Danielle Hébert – Saz

ADRENALIZED FREEDOM
Mona Seda – Vocals & Trumpet
Hector Rivera – Vocals & Guitar
Daniele De Cario – Bass
Forrest Robinson – Drums

Guitar re-amped by Shawn Lyon at his Studios in Los Angeles, California

9 798986 983301